CLAWS OF MURDER

LATTE'S MEWSINGS COZY MYSTERIES, BOOK 4

PATTI BENNING

SUMMER PRESCOTT BOOKS PUBLISHING

Copyright 2020 Summer Prescott Books

All Rights Reserved. No part of this publication nor any of the information herein may be quoted from, nor reproduced, in any form, including but not limited to: printing, scanning, photocopying, or any other printed, digital, or audio formats, without prior express written consent of the copyright holder.

**This book is a work of fiction. Any similarities to persons, living or dead, places of business, or situations past or present, is completely unintentional.

CHAPTER ONE

Lorelei French gazed out the coffee shop's front windows, mourning the long past summer days when it was still light out during closing. Even though they weren't open that late into the evening, it had already been pitch black outside for weeks when closing time rolled around. It made her evenings at home feel shorter, somehow, and even though it didn't make any logical sense, it took more effort for her to get her grocery shopping and her household chores done when it was dark outside, compared to when the sun was still shining and the birds were still whistling in the trees.

The beautiful, multicolored Christmas lights that seemed to cover every available vertical surface in town, from the streetlight poles to tree trunks, went a long way to make up for it. It had snowed recently enough that the snowdrifts lining the streets were still white, and that, along with the Christmas tree standing in the corner of the coffee shop and the festive tunes playing softly over the radio probably could have lifted even a dead man's spirits. Still, while Lorelei was glad for the Christmas cheer, she missed the sun.

"Sorry, Padraic, but we're just not looking for anyone else right now. Why don't you check back in the spring? Mary usually works fewer hours in the spring and summer, so we might have room for you to pick up a few."

"That's all well and good come spring, but I need something now," Padraic said. He shifted, shoving his hands into his coat pockets and glaring at the counter from under his wool hat. "I know I wasn't the best employee in the past, but that will change this time. I promise."

"You're not just asking me to give you a second chance," Lorelei said. "You're asking me to give you a third or fourth chance. It's not even that you were late occasionally. I could forgive that. It's that you have completely no showed to multiple shifts, you didn't even call in to tell us you were going to be gone. I can't ask my other employees to put up with that. Especially not now, when we're so busy. I'm not even saying I won't ever give you another chance. But it's going to have to wait until spring. I'm not going to cut other people's hours for you, not when you've already had so many chances."

"Come on," Padraic said, giving her his best pitiful look. "It's almost Christmas. Even just a few weeks of work would help. That's all I need."

"Sorry," Lorelei said again. She felt bad, but she had let Padraic go a couple of months ago and wasn't yet ready to give him another chance. He had a long history of being unreliable, and it simply wasn't fair to everyone else. It was a shame, because she liked him other than that, and when he actually showed up to work, he got the job done and was a favorite of the customers. "Why don't you check at some of the other little shops around town? Most places that are in the retail business are going to need temp employees during the holidays."

"Everyone has already filled the positions," he said,

blowing a breath out slowly. "I'll have to keep looking, though. Thanks anyway."

She watched him slouch toward the door, guilt nibbling at her innards, but she made herself hold firm. She was a forgiving employer, but at the end of the day she did run a business, and she couldn't hire someone who she knew would eventually no-show with no warning.

He let the door shut behind him, the little bell jingling to signify his departure. Lorelei sat back on her stool, sighing. Maybe she should just give him one more chance. She could hire him until Christmas, make sure he knew it was a seasonal position – no. Everyone wanted more hours, not fewer. She had to do right by Henry, Norah, Mary, and Jenny. They were all good, reliable employees and hard workers who gave their all to the coffee shop whenever they were there, and she wasn't about to cut their hours just because she felt bad for someone else.

Behind her, the door to the kitchen opened and Jenny came out, her blonde hair pulled back into a tight ponytail. "It's about time to start closing. Do you want me to –" She broke off, her gaze landing on the single occupied table in the corner. "Oh, I didn't realize we still had a customer. I'll start wiping down the other tables, if you'd like."

Lorelei shook herself, pushing away thoughts of Padraic and Christmas and early sunsets, and focusing on the task at hand.

"Go ahead. I'll start closing in the kitchen – we still have some of those croissants left, don't we? You can take them home if you'd like."

"Oh, no, I took some home yesterday," Jenny replied. "You should take them – Hugh is picking you up, right? You could just give them to him."

"Good idea. He always gets so happy when I give him something on the house."

Jenny giggled. "It's true what they say, about food being the way to a man's heart."

"Well, if I'm being honest, food is a pretty good way to my heart too," Lorelei said, sharing a grin with her younger employee.

Earlier in the day, their cheerful banter would have continued, but this close to closing time, both of them shared the desire to get their duties finished and head home as soon as possible. Lorelei ducked back into the kitchen, propping the door open so Jenny could come in and out to grab cleaning supplies or a clean rag easily if she needed to. Lorelei began wiping down the counters and putting away the dishes that were drying in the rack above the sink. She tucked the two remaining croissants into a box and placed them next to her purse so she would remember to give them to Hugh.

From the dining area, she heard Jenny say, "Bye, Wilson. We'll see you next week."

She heard the young man say something in return and the bell above the door jingled as he left. Jenny's voice came again a second later.

"No, Latte, you can't go out there. I don't think your mom wants to chase you through the snow all night. She's got a date with a handsome guy waiting for her after work."

Lorelei couldn't help but smile at that. Latte, her green eyed, brown furred Havana Brown, went to work with her most days. She had a cat bed on the windowsill out front and spent most of her time curled up in it, enjoying the sunlight and the occasional attention from the customers. Her employees all doted on the cat, and Lorelei had had to set some strict rules in place to keep them from giving her too many treats. Like all cats, Latte knew how to take advantage of her adoring fans.

Jenny came into the kitchen a few moments later, dropping the dirty rags into the laundry bag. "Do you want me to do the mopping?" she asked.

Lorelei waved her off. "No, you can head home if you'd like. Hugh won't be here for another ten or fifteen minutes, and that will give me enough time to finish up closing by myself. I'm going to make us some coffee for the road, too, so I'm not in any hurry."

"Are you sure? I feel bad leaving you to finish this on your own."

"I'm sure. Besides, you've got to walk home, don't you? The sooner you leave, the sooner you'll get there."

Jenny glanced toward the door and made a face at the icy darkness waiting for her. "You're right. It will be nice to be home a little bit sooner. Thanks, Lorelei."

"Be careful. Some of the sidewalks might be icy –

according to my phone, the temperature dropped quite a bit in the past couple of hours."

"I will be. I'll see you this weekend."

Lorelei watched Jenny leave through the front door, pausing to block Latte from following her. The bell jingled as she shut the door, and Latte stared out through the glass at the falling snow.

"Hugh will be here soon," Lorelei told the cat. "And I'd better get to work if I want to get everything done before he arrives. You keep watch for him."

She had just finished up the closing routine and was putting together the two cups of coffee for her and Hugh – she still had to clean the machines, but that would only take a minute – when the front door slammed open.

Expecting to see Hugh, she looked up to chastise him for opening the door so violently. Instead, she spotted Jenny, her cheeks and nose red with the cold, her hat pulled down over her hair, and her eyes wide with fright.

"Thank goodness you're still here. It was so horrible, I saw his blood on the snow –"

"Jenny, slow down," Lorelei said, coming out from behind the counter and approaching her employee. "What happened? Whose blood did you see?"

"Wilson – he was walking ahead of me, he must've stopped in at a store to pick something up because I know he left a few minutes before I did, but he was only about half a block in front of me. Someone just stepped out between two buildings and attacked him without any warning. I was frozen – I couldn't do anything. I ran away as soon as it was safe."

"He was attacked? Did you call the police?" Lorelei asked. She looked her terrified employee up and down. "Are you okay?"

"I'm okay," Jenny panted. "I don't think the man with the knife even saw me. But no, I didn't call the police. I was terrified that he was going to come after me next. I just ran as fast as I could, and this was the first place I thought of."

"Okay, sit down. I'll grab the phone and put the call in to 911, but you might need to talk to the dispatcher yourself."

"Can I lock the door first?" Jenny asked. "I'm just – what if he *did* follow me?"

PATTI BENNING

"Of course," Lorelei said soothingly. "You lock the front door. I'll lock the back, okay?"

Her employee nodded, tears beginning to brim in her eyes. Lorelei hurried into the kitchen to turn the lock on the delivery door, then grabbed the landline from its cradle out front and dialed the emergency number. Jenny sat down at a table, her hands still in their gloves and cradled in front of her.

Lorelei explained what happened to the dispatcher, then handed the phone over to Jenny, who told the story herself in a broken, unsure voice. Lorelei moved toward the windows, spotting Latte sitting in her cat bed, watching the proceedings with a judgmental look in her eyes. She felt her stomach swoop as she remembered the two times Latte had tried to leave the building after Wilson left.

"You knew, didn't you?" Lorelei asked, moving over to the cat to run her hand through her soft fur. "I'm so sorry. I was distracted, I didn't see the signs – you were trying to follow him, weren't you? If I had been paying more attention, we might have been able to save him."

Or we might have gotten hurt ourselves, a little voice

in the back of her mind said. She did her best to ignore it. She didn't know for sure whether or not she and Latte could have made a difference to Wilson, but at least if they had tried, she wouldn't feel this regret and guilt.

CHAPTER TWO

"They said someone should be here soon," Jenny said. "They want us to stay inside and wait for the police to get here. They – they want to question me. Do you think I'll be in trouble? For not trying to help him?"

"No, I don't," Lorelei said, turning back to her employee. "You said he was almost half a block ahead of you, and that the other man attacked him without warning. What could you have done? You wouldn't have stood a chance against someone armed with a knife."

"I still should have tried," Jenny said. "You would have."

Lorelei opened her mouth, then shut it again. Jenny wasn't wrong, but then Lorelei's experiences with Latte and all the people she had already saved had changed her. Before she could come up with an argument to make the younger woman feel better, Jenny's eyes widened and she pointed past Lorelei, toward the door.

"It's him! He followed me!"

Lorelei whirled around, then relaxed when she recognized the figure standing outside the door. It was Hugh, in his light brown coat, with a blue knit hat pulled down over his ears. He had his hand on the door handle and looked puzzled that it wouldn't open for him.

"It's just Hugh," she said as she moved toward the door. Behind her, Jenny gave a shaky laugh.

"Sorry. I'm jumpy."

"Don't worry, I don't blame you," she replied. She reached for the deadbolt and turned it, pulling the door open to let Hugh in. As soon as he stepped inside, she shut the door and turned the deadbolt back over.

"What's going on?" he asked, looking between the two of them. "Did something happen?"

"Come into the kitchen with me," Lorelei said. "I'll explain it back there. Shoot, I forgot to finish the coffee."

He followed her back to the counter, where she grabbed the two freshly poured cups of coffee. She handed him his and gestured toward the fridge. "There's cream in there, and we've got sugar on the counter. Flavor it however you want. Sorry, when Jenny came back in, I got distracted."

"What's going on?" he asked again, making his way to the refrigerator.

"Jenny witnessed an attack." In the silence after she spoke, she could hear sirens drawing nearer.

"The police are on their way. She's pretty shaken up, though."

"That's horrible," he said. He put his coffee down, looking a bit sick. "Was it someone she knew? Are they okay?"

"It was a regular, a man who comes to the coffee shop

frequently. We all know him by name, but I don't think she knew him other than that. And no – I don't think he's okay. She didn't stick around to see the aftermath, but from what she said, it sounded pretty bad."

"I can't imagine witnessing something like that," he said with a shudder. "I'm glad she's okay, though."

"Me too," Lorelei said. "Are you all right to wait back here for a little while? It sounds like the police are here. Jenny said they were going to send someone to talk to her, and I want to be available in case she needs me."

"Of course," he said. "We can do our shopping another day – I'll wait here as long as you need me to."

"Thank you."

She gave him a quick smile, then ducked back out into the dining area just in time to see Jenny unlock the door and let the police officer in. She could see flashing lights down the street; the other emergency responders seemed to have found the site of the attack.

They took a couple of minutes to introduce themselves, then the officer sat down with Jenny and Lorelei decided to finish cleaning the coffee machines, but kept half an ear tuned to their conversation. She paid the most attention when Jenny described the attacker; she hadn't wanted to press the younger woman for the description before, but she was curious to hear what he looked like.

"I don't know," Jenny said, when the officer asked her about him. "He could have been anyone. He was wearing his hood up, and I think he had a hat on under it. He had a black coat, and it looked like he was wearing dark pants. I think he had gloves on, but that's all I could really see. I was too far away to get a look at his face, and with his coat zipped it all the way up it would have been hard to see him anyway. I'm pretty sure he was a man, though. Just the way he moved, and how strong he was when he... when he attacked Wilson."

Her voice broke, and the officer paused to let her gather herself.

"Do you think you would recognize him if you saw his picture?"

She shook her head. "Sorry, but no. I... Well, for a second I thought he looked right at me. That's when I ran. Do you think I'm in danger?"

"Like you said, you were far away, and I'm guessing you were wearing winter gear as well, am I correct?" he asked. She nodded. "Then I don't think it's likely that he recognized you, but you should still keep aware of yourself and your surroundings and take precautions like locking your doors and not going anywhere alone at night for a while. If you ever feel like you're in danger, give the station a call and we will send a unit out to your location immediately."

"Thank you," she said.

The officer only had a couple of questions for Lorelei, mostly just asking about Wilson's behavior before he left that evening. Had he been acting strangely? Did he seem worried or frightened? Did he give any indication that he thought someone might be after him? She answered no to all of his questions. Wilson was a regular, and he hadn't acted any different than he usually does, unless paying with a hundred counted. He'd been in good cheer, and hadn't seemed to have a clue his time was limited.

Just as the police officer was preparing to leave, another knock came at the front door. Lorelei looked over and this time she recognized Deborah from the diner across the street, her tall shoulders hunched against the cold. Raising her eyebrows, she hurried over to let the other woman in.

Deborah stepped past her, shivering as the door shut on a snowy gust. "Sorry for interrupting, but I saw the flashing lights and I wanted to make sure you were okay."

"Thanks," Lorelei said, touched. "But we're fine. There was an attack down the road."

"Oh, dear. Is everyone all right?"

"The man who was attacked isn't," Lorelei said. "It was Wilson – Wilson Belgrove."

"You're not serious. Wilson?"

"Yes. Did you know him?"

"I did. He used to work for me. I had to let him go just last week. Oh, dear, I feel terrible. We didn't part on the best of terms, but I never wanted anything like this to happen."

"If you knew him, maybe you should talk to the police. You would know better than me if he had anything strange going on in his life. From the questions they were asking me, I think they're trying to figure out whether the person who attacked him knew him, or if it was a crime of convenience."

"I will. Whatever I can do to help."

By the time the officer was done questioning them and they were free to go, Lorelei's coffee had gotten cold. She stuck it in the microwave — something she always hated to do because it never tasted the same afterward — and let it warm her hands as she walked outside with Hugh. He was carrying Latte's cat carrier. The cat was crouched inside it on her bed, looking displeased at the flurry of snow that came rushing in at her through the bars.

"I'm sorry shopping didn't work out," she said as he put the cat carrier in the backseat.

"We can go shopping anytime," he said. "I just feel terrible that you and Jenny had to go through that. I'll take you and Latte straight home – I'm sure you want to rest."

"Are you sure? I feel bad, you came out here to pick us up just so we could do our Christmas shopping together."

"I'm sure." He paused while he got into the car, and she mirrored him on the other side. "Don't worry. It's not like I had to drive very far to come and get you, and besides, I dropped you off here this afternoon, I could hardly just leave you to find your own way home. I'm glad I'm picking you up, actually; with the roads this bad, you shouldn't be driving that convertible of yours anyway."

"I have snow tires on it," she said. "But thank you; maybe we can go this weekend."

"Saturday afternoon works for me. You usually work Saturday mornings, right?"

"You're right. We'll plan on that, then. I should be out by three." She frowned. "Actually, that's just in two days, and Jenny was supposed to work the afternoon shift with Norah. I'll have to see if she feels up to coming in. If she needs a little bit of extra time, I want her to take it."

"Yeah." He frowned. At first, Lorelei thought he was

just concentrating, since he was pulling out of the parking lot and onto the main road, but he still didn't say anything as he headed toward her house.

"What is it?" she asked after the silence dragged on for a few minutes.

"It's nothing," he said with a terse shake of his head.

"Obviously something is going on," she said. He turned onto a street only a block away from her house and she sighed. "If you're upset that I'm canceling the shopping trip, just tell me. I know how busy everything will be this weekend. It's going to be terrible."

"I'm not upset about that," he said. He relented with a sigh. "It's just... How do you always get mixed up in stuff like this, Lorelei? You've been involved, sometimes under very strange circumstances, when someone either died or was about to die too many times for me to keep discounting it. Every time it happens, I tell myself it was just a coincidence, but then it happens again.

"It is just a coincidence," she said, the lie tasting bitter on her tongue. "What do you think? That I'm involved with hurting those people somehow?"

"Of course not," he said, turning to look at her in honest shock. He jerked his gaze back to the road when the car hit a patch of ice and didn't speak until they were past it. "No, Lorelei, I would never think something like that. I know I've only known you a few months, but I come to the coffee shop almost every day, and we go out to eat together at least once a week. You're my best friend in town, and I don't know if you can call what we're doing dating since we've never had that discussion, but either way I still think I've gotten to know you pretty well. I just can't shake the feeling that there's something you're not telling me. Something important. And if it's because you don't trust me, just say it. At least admit that there is something there. My feelings might be hurt, but at least I'll stop feeling like I'm going crazy."

He risked a glance over at her again, but she couldn't speak. Her throat felt thick, and her stomach twisted with an entirely different kind of guilt than what she had felt earlier in the coffee shop.

"There is... something," she said just as he turned into her driveway. "I can't tell you. Not yet. Not because I don't trust you, but because I know I'm going to sound crazy. I don't know how to prove it to you. But I promise, I'm not trying to hurt anyone. The opposite, in fact."

"Will you tell me, one day?" he asked quietly.

"Yes," she said, surprised to find that she meant it. "I will. I promise. I just… I need more time."

"Okay," he said. "Thank you. Let me know about Saturday, okay? Do you want me to stay for a bit? I know that guy Jenny saw attack the other man is still out there. I don't want you to feel frightened."

She gave him a weak smile. "It's okay. I've got Latte with me."

He glanced in the back, giving the cat a skeptical look, then shook his head with a laugh. "She does seem pretty loyal to you. I'd feel better if you had a big guard dog with you, but she'll do."

"Don't even think the D word around her," Lorelei said with a shiver. "Last time I made the mistake of wondering out loud whether or not I should get a dog, she wouldn't pay any attention to me for days."

Chuckling, and likely assuming she was joking, Hugh just got out of the car, opening the back door to grab Latte's cat carrier while Lorelei made sure she had her phone, purse, and keys. He carried the cat carrier up to the door for her and waited while she unlocked the deadbolt, then handed it over. She put the carrier down just inside the door and turned around to give Hugh a hug, stretching up to press a quick kiss to his cheek.

"Thanks, Hugh. You're wonderful. I really don't know what I would do without you. I'll make it up to you, I promise, and I'll let you know about Saturday as soon as I talk to Jenny."

"Call me if you need anything else tonight," he said. "And if not, I'll see you tomorrow, like usual."

"See you tomorrow. Drive safely on your way home."

She watched as he walked back toward his car, but the icy wind chased her inside sooner than she would have liked. With a sigh, she shut the door and crouched to let Latte out of her carrier. The cat slunk out, her tail twitching. Her whiskers had beaded moisture on them from the snowflakes, and when Lorelei reached down to pet her, her fur was the slightest bit damp. The cat moved away from her and jumped up on the low table where her food and water dishes were, glaring.

"Sorry, but there's no reason to be mad at me. It's not my fault it was snowing tonight."

She opened the closet and put the cat carrier on the floor inside, then took off her boots and her coat. Shutting the closet, she turned around and made her way to the cupboard where Latte's cans of food were kept. She selected one in the very back, a can of salmon patè with a creamy gravy, and popped the top open. Latte begin eating immediately when Lorelei poured the food into her bowl, her earlier annoyance pouring off her like water.

"You're easy to bribe," she said fondly. "Your fur will be dry by the time you're done eating, and besides, getting a little bit wet won't hurt you. Sometimes I think you're just the tiniest bit spoiled."

She thought again of the two times Latte had tried to leave the coffee shop right before Wilson was attacked and felt another surge of guilt. It was her job to be aware of those things. She had been distracted by closing out the coffee shop, but that was no excuse. Saving people's lives was much more important than closing on time.

Exhausted down to her very bones, Lorelei left Latte

to eat in peace and opened another cupboard, this time to take out a mug. It was her favorite Christmas mug; it featured Rudolph the reindeer, and had two branching handles off either side that were his antlers. It was cheerful and silly, and she had never been able to find another one like it.

She took a clean pot out of the drying rack on the right-hand side of her sink and measured some milk into it, then put it on the stove to heat up. In the pantry, she took out the container of hot chocolate mix and hesitated when she saw the marshmallows. After a moment's thought, she left them; tonight was a whipped cream sort of night.

Once the milk was simmering, she poured it into her mug and mixed in the hot cocoa, then gave herself a generous amount of whipped cream on top. She cleaned everything up, wanting to be able to relax completely once she was done, then took the mug into the living room and sat on the couch, kicking her feet up onto the coffee table. No sooner had the mug touched her lips than she put it down again, this time rising and going into the corner to turn on the Christmas tree lights. The multicolored glow made her heart glad, and this time when she sat on the couch, she felt some of the stress of the day beginning

PATTI BENNING

to seep away. She sipped her hot chocolate, wiped a dot of whipped cream off the tip of her nose, then grabbed the TV remote. A Christmas movie before bed would hopefully keep her mind off of the man that she hadn't been able to save.

CHAPTER THREE

"Ms. French, I've got something for you," Henry said when she came into the coffee shop the next morning. She was a little later than usual, having not slept well the night before, but thankfully Henry was more than capable of opening on his own.

Henry was her oldest employee, not oldest in the sense that he had worked there the longest, but literally the oldest person there. The sight of an elderly man carefully making lattes and mochas and macchiatos took some of her newer customers by surprise, since he didn't quite match the popular trend of young, perky baristas, but Henry knew most of the older contingent in town, and he had a way with coffee. Lorelei had never once regretted hiring him, and often wished that he would sign on full time.

"More bills?" she asked, assuming he was talking about the coffee shop's mail.

"Luckily for you, nope. Mrs. White at the bakery gave you something extra in the order this morning."

"Oooh." The promise of an unexpected tasty treat was a lot more encouraging than the thought of a bill that she had missed. She joined Henry over by the box of freshly made bagels that he brought to the coffee shop whenever he worked mornings. He had already unpacked most of them and put them in the display case, but there was a single perfect cinnamon brown sugar bagel waiting for her inside. She could feel her mouth watering already, and hurried over to the toaster oven to turn it on.

"She sent some of that cinnamon cream cheese spread you like so much, too," he said.

"I'm going to have to send her a Christmas card with some coupons for free coffee," Lorelei said "Did you want some of the bagel? I don't mind sharing."

"She slipped me a Swiss cheese and bacon bagel on

the way out," he said with a wink. "This sugary monstrosity is all yours."

Cheered by Mrs. White's kindness and a healthy dose of sugar and carbs, Lorelei hummed her way through the morning. Their current special, Peppermint Foam Mocha, was a huge hit with her customers. It was chocolatey and minty, with just a dash of peppermint flavoring added to the whipped cream before she made it to give it an unexpected hit of flavor. She sprinkled ground dark chocolate and crushed candy cane on top of each one, and had received a myriad of compliments about it in just the last few days alone. She was tempted to keep it going past Christmas, but she had a couple ideas that she wanted to try out for the New Year's special. She didn't get very many opportunities to use edible glitter, after all.

As the hours passed, the darkness outside lifted and the sun rose, revealing it to be a clear day. The sunlight sparkled off of the snow outside, and Lorelei was just about to poke her head into the kitchen to ask Henry if he had salted the parking lot yet when the front door opened and Alyssa came in.

"Trick-or-treat," her best friend said.

"Wrong holiday," Lorelei replied with a grin. "And no, before you ask, I haven't gotten any more marshmallow fluff or candy corn. You're going to have to wait until next year to have another Candy Mallow Latte. And that's if I even bring it back. I've been told by multiple people that it was an abomination."

"They don't know what they're talking about," Alyssa grumbled. "That drink was ambrosia. Pure sugar. The orange colored whipped cream was a nice touch."

"It's the last time I'm ever letting you help me come up with a special," Lorelei said. "You do realize that roughly two-thirds of the population hates candy corn, right?"

"It was the perfect Halloween drink, and I'm always going to mourn its passing." Alyssa leaned against the counter with a dramatic sigh, letting her forehead rest against the cool surface.

"It's been almost two months. Shouldn't you be in the acceptance stage of grief by now? Try one of the new mochas. I'll even add extra chocolate on top."

"I'm not ready for it to be Christmas yet," her friend

groaned. "Can't I just be in denial a little while longer?"

"You love Christmas."

"Right. That's why I don't want it to almost be over. Where did the year go? You know what comes after Christmas? Winter. Months and months of nothing but cold, and snow, and ice, with no holidays to look forward to."

"You poor thing," Lorelei said dryly. "I feel so bad for you."

Alyssa straightened up to give her a mock glare. "I can hear the sympathy absolutely dripping from your voice. Come on, give me a caramel macchiato. I guess I'll have to go back to my old favorite."

"Coming right up."

"Not that I just came here to gossip, but is it true that you were here when Wilson Belgrove died? People are saying you witnessed the murder, but I told them that probably wasn't true. You would've called me if you had."

"It wasn't me; it was Jenny. Did you know him?"

PATTI BENNING

"Sort of. I used to live across from him. He moved out a little while ago; he and his roommate didn't get along. Still, it's strange to think that he is just… gone, now. Did they catch the guy who did it?"

"Not yet, as far as I know," she replied. She poured milk into a cup, then crouched down to open the mini fridge where the caramel was stored. "They've only had about a day to work on the case, though. Unfortunately, Jenny didn't get a good description of the guy, since he was all bundled up."

"So, it could be anyone," Alyssa said, shuddering. "Heck, it could even be my across the hall neighbor."

"His old roommate?"

Her friend nodded. "His name's Benny. He seems like an alright dude, but you never really know, do you? Let me tell you, he absolutely despised Wilson by the end of it. I don't blame him – I had to go over to their apartment once to borrow some sugar for my morning coffee – sorry to burst your bubble, but I do sometimes make my own coffee instead of coming here – and the place was a mess. Benny told me it was all Wilson's stuff, and he'd given up trying to clean up after the guy. I stopped in just a couple days ago to return his carpet cleaner and the place was spotless, so I know Benny was telling the truth about Wilson being the messy one. According to Benny, Wilson skipped out on the last month of rent too. He didn't give him any notice; he just up and left as soon as he found a new place to live. Benny never really pursued it since he was just so glad Wilson was gone."

"Wow. He always seemed nice and normal when he came in here. Though Deborah did mention that he stole some money from her cash register."

"Diner Deborah?" Alyssa asked, her eyes going wide at the new gossip.

"I wish you wouldn't call her that," Lorelei said, rolling her eyes. She poured the coffee, then handed the finished drink over to her friend. "It's not like we know any other Deborahs."

"There are other Deborahs in town. Probably. I'm just saving us some confusion for when we meet them. And there was the Deborah this Deborah bought the diner from. Technically she's Diner Deborah, version two."

"You just don't like her," Lorelei replied. "You're still holding that grudge from when she spilled orange juice on your new skirt. And yes, it was her. He used to work there, apparently."

"See? People can seem normal on the outside, but inside they're messy, thieving people who don't pay their rent."

"Well, considering that Wilson was murdered, I'm not sure it's fair to talk poorly about him. Even if he liked to leave his dirty dishes lying around and stole some cash, it doesn't mean he deserved to die."

"No, of course not. You're right; I need to remember that is an actual person who stopped living, not just someone I've heard stories about. Now that you've made me feel like a terrible person, let's talk about something else. How's it going with Hugh?"

"The same as it has been," Lorelei replied. "I feel like I've been friend zoned. Does that happen to women? Or maybe he thinks I friend zoned him. Nothing has really changed in the past month. We go out to eat together once or twice a week, we hold hands some-times, he'll kiss my cheek or I'll kiss his, and of course we talk a lot. I just sometimes doubt that he wants more."

"You know I'm always on your side, but to be fair, you have been rather... distracted lately."

"What do you mean?"

"I'm not sure how to explain it, exactly. But for the past couple of months, you've seemed to have your mind on something else. If I was dating you, I'd probably take it as a sign that you aren't very interested."

"That's not it at all," Lorelei said. "Is that really how it looks from the outside?"

"That's how it seems to me," Alyssa said with a shrug. "But I know you well enough to figure that if you want to talk about whatever's going on, you'll tell me. I'd pry if I thought it was good for you, but you don't seem upset, really. Just... not all there all the time."

"Well, thanks for telling me. I'm not trying to be distant to anyone. I'll work on it."

"I'll let you know how you do," Alyssa said cheerfully. "So, what special are you going to offer for New Year's?"

Lorelei leaned closer to her friend, lowering her

voice. "You're going to love this. Two words; edible glitter."

The bright, eager look in her friend's eyes and slightly too loud squeal made her smile. She would never be as perpetually cheerful as Alyssa was, but sometimes just basking in all of the energy did wonders to make her feel better.

CHAPTER FOUR

Lorelei pushed her curtain to the side, peering out the window and into the darkness. Across the street, a single orange streetlight lit up a circle of sidewalk, but her gaze was drawn to the car parked in the shadows just beyond the light. Just barely, she could make out the outline of a person inside.

Or at least, she thought it was a person. There was a slight possibility that she was going insane and it was just an oddly shaped bush on the other side of the car that happened to be perfectly positioned to look like a person when she looked through the car's windows, but she was pretty sure she had seen the figure move the last time she looked. And if it was a person, then they had been sitting there for the past half an hour, and they were watching her house.

Normally, she wasn't so paranoid, but during the last part of her shift, she could have sworn someone was watching her and Jenny, and on her way home, she thought she had seen a car following her. Then she had pulled into her driveway and saw the car go on its way and felt silly, but that hadn't shaken the feeling of being watched for long and the next time she looked out the window, a car was parked where there hadn't been one before.

While she was watching, a pair of headlights cut through the darkness. Whoever was sitting in the car leaned back against the seat. She felt a thrill of fear mixed with a sense of justification. Someone was definitely there.

The car slowed, then pulled into her driveway. She waited until the headlights shut off and she recognized the vehicle as Hugh's before grabbing her purse.

"I'll be back later, Latte."

She stepped outside, pausing to lock the door behind her as Hugh walked up to her front porch.

"Ready to go?" he asked.

"Yep. Where do you want to start?"

"We can head to the antique store first. I think we've both got people we have to buy gifts for who would like something from there, right?"

"Probably. My mom likes weird collectibles. I'll have to get something for Allison, too, and each of the employees."

"We don't have to get everything tonight, but I'd like to at least make a dent in it." He walked with her down to the car, then opened the passenger door for her. As she got in, he made a face. "Don't tell anyone, but I absolutely hate Christmas shopping."

She waited until he got in on the other side, then replied, "I like it if the person is easy to shop for, like Alyssa, but for some people, it's impossible to find the perfect gift."

Like you, she thought but didn't say. She still had to buy Hugh his gift, and had absolutely no idea what she was going to get him. A new camera? He was a professional photographer. Any camera he would be interested in would be way out of her budget, and she wouldn't even know where to begin. The same applied to any accessories for his camera, and it wasn't as though she could get him something generic, like a candle. There were people out there who really liked getting candles, but it would just feel like a copout if she gave one to him.

He pulled out of the driveway, turning left, away from the car where her stalker was. She turned in her seat to watch the other vehicle as they drove away. Sure enough, only moments later, the vehicle's headlights turned on and it pulled onto the road after them. She turned to face forward, sliding her eyes over to Hugh.

"Don't freak out, but I think someone's following me," she said softly.

Despite her warning, he jerked the wheel slightly, making the car swerve. "What? Why didn't you say something earlier?" She saw his eyes dart up to the rearview mirror. "Is it the car behind us?"

"Yes. They were sitting in their car outside of my house for about half an hour, and I swear someone was watching me before I ended my shift at the coffee shop."

"Do you think it's the same person?"

"I don't know. It's hard to see what sort of vehicle it is in the dark. I thought someone was following me on my way home, but I think I was just being paranoid then. I might have been imagining things earlier, but this person was definitely waiting outside my house."

"Do you have your cell phone on you? Do you want to call the police?"

"I do, but I'm not sure what I'd say. Part of me thinks that this whole thing with Jenny has got me spooked. I know there's someone out there who committed murder just a couple days ago; is my subconscious afraid of him? Is my brain making connections where there aren't any just because I'm afraid he's going to be waiting around the corner?"

"I'm going to drive around the block. If the car is still behind us when we get back to this road, we'll know that they're following us – there's no good reason for them to drive around the block otherwise. If they are, you should call the police and I'll begin driving toward the police department. If they don't follow us, we can figure it's probably just a coincidence that they left the same time we did."

"All right," she said. "I'll keep watch on them."

He turned on his blinker, slowing as they reached the end of the block. After stopping at the stop sign, he looked both ways, then turned right. Lorelei turned in her seat, her heart pounding as she waited. She watched as the other vehicle pulled up to the stop sign. There was a pause, then it turned right, keeping up behind them.

She and Hugh rode in silence until they reached the end of the block once again. He turned, and just like before, the other vehicle turned as well. Her breath gusted out of her, fogging the window. She wiped it clean with her sleeve, then found the knob of the door lock and made sure it was down.

"Two more turns," he said.

"What if they figure out what we're doing? What if they ambush us or something?"

"If they try to get ahead of us, I'll just speed up. We're close to downtown; I don't think they would do anything in public."

He reached the stop sign and put on his blinker. Lorelei waited with bated breath while he turned, watching behind them for the other vehicle. It paused at the stop sign, then rolled through the intersection, going straight.

She breathed out a sigh of relief and turned back around. "I guess I was just imagining things."

"They probably just stopped on a side street to look up directions, and it just happened to be across from your house," he said. "I believe you that they were outside of your house for a while, though. I can see how that would be disconcerting, especially after what you and Jenny went through the other night. I think you should call the police if you see them again, though. It's possible they figured out that we knew they were following us and decided they didn't want to draw attention anymore."

She shuddered. "Well, either way, I'm glad that they stopped for now. Let's focus on our Christmas shopping; there is nothing I can do about the person in the car right now anyway, and I don't want our evening to be ruined."

They didn't see the person in the car or any signs that someone was following her again for the rest of the night. Since it was a Saturday evening and the holidays were right around the corner, a lot of the little shops in town had extended hours. There was a super-market about half an hour away, and some larger chain stores as well, but she preferred shopping at the small, locally owned stores where she knew the people who ran them by name. Hugh felt the same way; he hadn't been in Wildborne as long as Lorelei had, but he had fallen in love with the little, picturesque town, and was even more diligent than she was about supporting local businesses.

Their decision to stop at the antique shop first ended up being a good one; she found something not only for her mother, but also for Hugh – she slipped it out of sight before he could see it, and asked the woman behind the register to hold it for her when he was on the other side of the store.

Finding something small for her employees wasn't too hard either, but even though Alyssa was easy to shop for, she still hadn't found the perfect gift for her. She spotted a lot of things her friend would enjoy, but she wanted to give her something really meaningful this year. *And here I thought Hugh was going to be the hard one to shop for,* she thought, grinning to herself as they got back into his car a few hours later.

CLAWS OF MURDER

She was looking forward to getting home and wrapping the gifts, because afterward, they would go under the tree. It was hardly Christmas without gifts under the tree, and she already had a few small things for Latte wrapped and piled up under the boughs.

Hugh slowed down as he neared her house. "Do you want me to drive around the block after I drop you off and see if I can see that car?"

"That would make me feel better," she admitted, touched that he had thought of it. "I wish I'd gotten a better view of the vehicle. I'm going to be so jumpy for the next few days."

"You should get someone to come stay with you. Alyssa, maybe. Or I could stay – I don't mind sleeping on the couch."

"I do have a guestroom," she pointed out. "I think I'll be fine tonight, though. I'm not actually sure that person was following me – I could just be jumping to all the wrong conclusions. I don't see why somebody would go to the effort of stalking me like that. But if he comes back, I might take you up on that offer."

"I'll make sure I keep my phone's volume up tonight," he said. He pulled into the driveway and left the car running while he got out, walking her up to the house. He looked around, seeming to be on guard against whatever might be lurking in the darkness. She smiled and let herself enjoy the feeling of someone looking out for her. The fact that he cared so much about her well-being was touching, even when neither of them was completely sure there was actually anything to be worried about.

He held her bags as she unlocked the door, and they said their goodbyes. He walked back down the steps as she stepped inside, nudging the door open with her hip so she could drop her bags off on the counter, maneuvering them carefully in order not to break anything inside. While she was putting the bags down, a dark blur ran across the floor and slipped past her feet and out the door. Lorelei jumped and turned toward the fleeing form of her cat reflexively, but had to twist back around to catch a bag that had nearly slipped off the edge of the counter. By the time she turned back around, Latte had vanished into the darkness, and Hugh was already pulling onto the road.

CHAPTER FIVE

She thought about calling him, she really did. She knew he had his cell phone on him, and he would be happy to turn around and help her find the cat. The only problem was, she still wasn't quite ready to explain to him the truth about what Latte could do. No, this was something that she had to handle on her own.

With a sigh, she grabbed her purse and stepped back outside, locking the door behind her.

"Latte?" she called out softly, hoping that the cat had simply darted outside to chase a bird or an imagined mouse.

Latte usually came when she was called, though not

with the same speed or eagerness to please as a dog. When the seconds ticked by with no sign of the cat, she sighed and began trudging toward her car. It had snowed while they were out, just a dusting, but it was enough that she had to scrape the snow off of her windows and mirrors before getting in. The convertible was freezing inside; its soft top was not ideal for the cold weather. As she did every winter, she wondered why she didn't just sell the thing and get something a bit more useful. Come summer, though, she knew she would be glad that she still had it.

She started the engine and while it warmed up, she pulled out her cell phone and opened the application that linked to the GPS collar that Latte wore. The cat wasn't far away, but she was moving quickly. Even as Lorelei watched, the screen updated with her new position. She wasn't ambling along or even trotting quickly like she sometimes did– at this speed, she must be flat out running.

Seized with concern that whoever Latte had sensed was at the end of their time was going to meet their fate soon, she pulled out of the driveway and turned down the road, heading the same direction the cat had gone.

During Latte's wanderings, she usually stuck to the sidewalks or went through the trees or parks. She was exceedingly smart for a cat, and seem to inherently understand the dangers of a road. So, when Lorelei spotted her running down the middle of the street, she knew immediately that something was different this time.

She pulled the car as close to the cat as she dared and stopped the vehicle, turning her hazards on and then hopping out and running after Latte. Her blinkers lit up the road strangely, the light shining off of the snow and making the entire street seemed to glow intermittently. Latte paused, turning to look at her when she called out. Lorelei crouched down, reaching out for the cat but not wanting to look like she was chasing her.

"Come here, girl. We can go together in the car. It will be safer than running down the road, and a lot faster too. Come on, Latte. All the salt on the road can't be good for you – if you keep doing this, I'm going to have to wash your paws off when we get home."

That seemed to do it. Latte approached slowly, moving stiffly with her tail twitching. It was partially fluffed up, and her eyes caught the lights from the car, reflecting them back at Lorelei. She looked like some strange, wild creature for a second, but a moment later her cheek rubbed against Lorelei's fingers and Lorelei scooped the warm cat up into her arms, jogging back to her car. She deposited Latte on the passenger seat, and turned off her hazards and put the vehicle into drive, heading the same direction Latte had been running.

Latte climbed up onto the dashboard, crouching there and watching intently out the window. Lorelei neared the end of the block and glanced at the cat, wondering which way they were supposed to go. Suddenly, Latte darted from the front of the vehicle to the back, putting her paws up on the top of the back seat and looking out the back window, her tail twitching in agitation.

"What's going on?" Lorelei asked. "I thought we were supposed to be going this way?"

The cat gave a single meow, which didn't do much to explain the situation. Lorelei pulled over and was about to find a place to turn around when she spotted headlights in the rearview mirror. She turned, watching the vehicle approach. Latte watched as well as it got closer and closer, her gaze never once flickering. Lorelei felt her heart rate increase. Was this her stalker?

The vehicle slowed as it drew even with her car, and she realized with a jolt of relief that it was Hugh. Of course, he had said he was going to drive around the block, hadn't he?

She saw him roll down his passenger side window, so she rolled down her window so she could speak to him.

"Lorelei? What are you doing out here?"

"Latte slipped out the door, I had to go and get her," she said, gesturing to the cat in the back. She glanced back as she did so, and to her surprise she saw that Latte was sitting calmly on the seat, licking one of her back legs as if nothing had happened.

Had the person that they were supposed to save died? Or had she somehow already managed to change their fate?

Before Hugh could reply, a vehicle blasted across the intersection, running the stop sign and going at least twenty miles over the speed limit. She could hear the tires screeching as the car slowed to take the curve further down the road, and she glanced over at Hugh, her eyes wide. They were both silent.

"If I hadn't stopped to talk to you, they might have hit me," he said, his face pale. "No one gets that lucky. This isn't the first time you've stopped something terrible from happening to me."

"I really just came out here to look for Latte," she said. She knew her own eyes were wide, and her heart was pounding. It was starting to make sense – Latte had started running the same direction Hugh had gone, but when he circled around the block, he had ended up behind them. And no wonder Latte had been in such a rush. Hugh would have been hit by that car just minutes after dropping her off if he hadn't pulled over to talk to her.

"I don't know what to say," he said. "I – I guess I owe you again. Thank you. Even if you didn't mean to, you saved my life. Again."

"Right." She stared at the road where the car had sped past, her mind still whirling with how close Hugh had come to being in a very serious accident.

"Lorelei? Are you okay?"

"Yes, I just – I'd better head home now. Sorry, I'm pretty shaken up by this. I know you probably are too – are you okay?"

"I'm fine, thanks to you. Are you going to be okay going home alone? Do you want me to come with you?"

"No. I'm going to be fine. I might take a bath or something. That was just… Really close. I'm glad you recognized my car and stopped to see what I was doing."

"I guess it's a good thing you have such a unique vehicle," he said, giving her a weak smile. "Oh, and before you ask; no, I didn't see anyone suspicious when I drove around the block. If you're sure you want to be alone tonight, I'll head home. I'll message you when I get there though – to let you know that I haven't had any other close calls."

"Okay. Thank you. Drive safely, Hugh."

She watched as he pulled forward, stopping at the stop sign. He stayed there for long seconds, and she imagined him carefully checking both ways twice before venturing forward. Once he had safely crossed the intersection, she did a U-turn and drove back down the block, pulling into her driveway and taking the cat into her arms.

She did not loosen her grip on Latte until the door to the house was shut and locked behind her. Instead of putting her on the ground, she carried her over to the sink and set her on the counter, keeping one hand on the cat's back to prevent her from jumping off while she found a clean rag. Wetting it, she squeezed the water out until it was just barely damp, then gently cleaned each of the cat's paws.

"You don't want to lick any of that road salt off," she told Latte as she worked. "It's probably got all sorts of chemicals in it. No more running in the roads, okay? I know you were just trying to get to Hugh in time, but it's dangerous, especially in the winter. Even if someone sees you, they may not be able to stop in time."

As she finished with each foot, the cat flicked it as if disgusted by the touch of water, her eyes narrowed with irritation, but when Lorelei took the bag of cat treats out of the cupboard, all was forgiven. After the cat ate her treats, Lorelei spent a couple of seconds petting her, then remembered her Christmas gifts. She wasn't exactly in the holiday mood anymore, but wrapping them might make her feel better.

It bothered her, though, that Hugh found himself in danger so frequently. It wasn't as though he had a particularly dangerous job or made a lot of enemies. Was he just the unluckiest person in the entire world, or was there something else going on? Most of the time, she and Latte only had to intercede once, and if they succeeded, the person's life went on uninterrupted. The few times she'd had to step in more than once, it had been when a criminal was involved, someone who was determined to cause harm, but that wasn't what was happening with Hugh.

Not for the first time, she wished that she had someone to talk to about all of this. Right now, the only people who knew were Mr. Bath, the manager at the nursing home where Latte used to live, and her mother. Her mother had warmed up to Latte somewhat, but still didn't like any mention of the cat's special nature. Mr. Bath grudgingly took up the mantle of helping Latte save people when Lorelei absolutely couldn't do it for some reason, but only because the cat had saved his life before and he felt like he owed them. Besides, he wasn't really one to philosophize about things.

What she really needed was someone to talk to who had gone through something similar themselves, but she had no way of knowing if there had ever even been any other cats like Latte. As far as she knew, Latte was completely unique.

CHAPTER SIX

The next morning, Lorelei got Latte bundled back up into her carrier and the two of them headed off to work together. The coffee shop opened a little bit later on Sundays, and closed a bit earlier, but just because the hours were shorter didn't mean it would be an easier day. Unlike the weekdays, it was the hours between ten and noon that were the busiest on Sundays – that was when most people were getting out of church, and the coffee shop and Deborah's Diner were tied for the two most popular places to go once worship was over.

She was the first one to arrive that morning, which wasn't unusual. She didn't start worrying until the clock began to edge toward eight-thirty and Jenny still hadn't shown up. It wasn't like the younger woman to be late, especially not this late. They all walked in two or three minutes past the start of their shift sometimes, even Lorelei, but Jenny was running almost twenty minutes behind schedule.

Taking advantage of the slow early mornings on Sundays, she waited until the coffee shop was empty then grabbed the phone and dialed in Jenny's number. Her employee picked up on what must have been the last ring.

"Oh, my goodness, Lorelei, I'm so sorry. I completely lost track of the time."

The panic in the younger woman's voice was the first thing she heard, and she immediately tried to calm her down. "You've never been this late before, Jenny. Don't worry, I'm not mad, I'm just concerned. Did something happen? Are you all right?"

"Someone broke into my apartment last night," Jenny said. Her voice broke on the last word. "I was out with a friend, and I saw the mess when I got home. I ended up going back to my friend's house to stay with her after the police left, but I decided to stop by the apartment this morning and grab some clean clothes for work. But then I started cleaning and trying to figure out if anything was missing, and I just completely forgot to check the time. I'm so, so sorry."

"Jenny, I'm more concerned with the fact that your apartment got broken into. Do you know who it was? Did they take anything important?"

"I… I'm not sure," Jenny said, but her tone seemed hesitant, as if she wasn't telling the whole truth. "I'll talk to you more when I get there – I'm going to head right over. I feel terrible. I'll stay late this afternoon if you need me to. I'll see you soon."

Her employee hung up before she could say anything. Lorelei sighed and put the phone down, wondering just what was going on with the younger woman. Jenny lived on a second-floor apartment; for someone to have broken in, either she had left the door unlocked, or they had broken it down. Lorelei highly doubted that Jenny had left the door unlocked just two days after witnessing one man kill another, which meant that whoever broken in likely used brute force. The question was, why? It seemed like a lot of effort for someone to go to for very little reward. She doubted Jenny owned anything of such value to make her apartment irresistible to a thief. Lorelei didn't even own anything that would put her in a high-risk category for a break-in, other than maybe her television and one or two small pieces of nice jewelry that few people had ever seen her wear.

Jenny must have left just seconds after ending the call with Lorelei, because she arrived at the coffee shop just minutes later, her cheeks flushed and her ponytail struggling to contain multiple frizzy flyaways. She looked frazzled, which Lorelei couldn't blame her for. She would look frazzled too if she was dealing with everything Jenny was.

"Jenny, you should have stayed on the line. I was going to tell you to take the day off if you need it."

"No, I'm not going to just duck out of a shift without notice like that, not unless I'm really sick or get in an accident or something," her employee said. She bustled into the kitchen and Lorelei had to turn aside to take a customer's order. Jenny reappeared a few minutes later, looking a bit more put together. She had her apron tied on, and had redone her ponytail. Lorelei finished serving the customer with a smile, then turned her attention back to her employee, her expression becoming more serious.

"Well, for future reference, I definitely consider dealing with a break-in a good enough reason to miss work. Do you want to talk about it, or would you rather think about something else for a while?"

"Honestly, I'm still in shock that it happened at all," Jenny said. She frowned at the display case, which was running low on everything bagels. "Whoever it was didn't take anything, other than my rainy-day jar, which was sitting out on my counter. It had a few bills and some change in it. Mostly, things were just destroyed. They… they spray-painted something on my wall too."

"What did they draw?" Lorelei asked, filled with morbid curiosity.

"A pair of lips, with an X through them," Jenny said softly.

Lorelei felt a thrill of realization run through her. "Jenny, that sounds like it's supposed to be a warning, or a threat."

"I know," her employee whispered. "The police took pictures of it but didn't really say much about it. I know who it's from, though. It's from the man who killed Wilson. I have no proof, but I'm dead positive about it, and I'm worried that next time he breaks in, I might be there."

Lorelei glanced around the room, making sure that they had privacy. There were only two women there, and they were talking loudly in the far corner. She lowered her voice to a whisper, matching Jenny's. "Are you sure you didn't recognize him? It sounds like he wants you to keep your mouth shut – which means he must think you know something."

"I swear I didn't see anything," Jenny whispered frantically. "All I saw was a person with a bunch of winter clothes on. It could have been an eighteen-year-old boy or a sixty-year-old woman for all I know."

"It's going to be okay, Jenny. Look, even if it really is a warning to keep your mouth shut, you're not going to say anything anyway – because you don't know anything. What are the police going to do?"

"They're going to do some drive-bys and crack down on local vandals," she said. "I'm not going to stay there again until my landlord fixes my door, though. I'll stay at a hotel or with a friend, somewhere I can feel safe."

"If you need any time off…" Lorelei began.

"No," Jenny said, shaking her head. She straightened up and brushed invisible wrinkles off of her apron. "I need the hours, especially now. I'm going to have to replace a lot of my stuff, and that won't be cheap. Plus, I feel a lot safer here, working with you, Henry, Mary, and Norah, than I would standing around in a motel room alone. Unless you think that I might be putting the coffee shop or you guys in danger. I don't want anyone else to get hurt."

"No, I'm not worried about that," Lorelei said. "I just want you to take care of yourself."

For a moment, she thought about telling Jenny about the person she thought was following her the night before. She decided against it, though. She didn't want to give the younger woman anything else to be concerned about, and she highly doubted that it was the same person. After all, she hadn't witnessed Wilson's murder. His killer had no reason to want her to keep quiet.

The door to the coffee shop opened, signaling that their time for private conversation was over. Jenny slipped into the back to get more bagels and start on the morning's muffins, and Lorelei turned to smile at Deborah, who looked dead tired as she approached the counter.

"I need something with a lot of sugar and caffeine," the other woman said. "Nothing with mint in it, though; the smells of mint coffee and frying egg just don't go together, and I've got to run over to the diner after this."

"You liked that raspberry caramel latte of ours, didn't you?" Lorelei asked. Deborah was one of her most frequent regulars – she owned the diner across the street and came in almost every day.

"I loved it, but I thought you weren't offering it anymore."

"Officially we aren't, but I think we've still got some of the flavoring in the back. I'll make you one of those with an extra shot of espresso. That should give you the boost that you need."

"Thank you, Lorelei, you are a lifesaver. You've got to stop in sometime and try our new corned beef hash. We're going to start making crepes as well, though probably not until after the holidays."

"I'll try to find the time sometime this week," Lorelei said. "I'll be right back – I've got to get that flavoring."

She found the rest of the raspberry flavoring and returned to the front to make the raspberry caramel latte. She gave it the extra shot of espresso, added whipped cream on top – Deborah had asked for all the sugar she could get, after all – and handed it over, slipping the bills that Deborah passed her into the register.

"Busy morning?" she asked.

"Busy night," Deborah said. "I'm just getting into work now, right in time for the rush."

Lorelei chuckled. "Well, good luck."

"You too," Deborah said, raising her latte in a farewell gesture.

As she left the building, Jenny poked her head out of the kitchen.

"Your cell phone is ringing."

"I'd better at least see who it is. Can you watch the counter?"

"Yep. I put the banana muffins in the oven a few minutes ago – they'll need to come out soon."

"I'll keep my eye on the timer," Lorelei promised.

They traded places, Jenny stepping behind the counter and Lorelei heading back into the kitchen, which smelled warm, like bananas and butter and roasting coffee. She dug through her purse, where her phone had fallen silent. There was one missed call from her mother and, after only a moment's hesitation, she called the older woman back. They weren't that busy at the coffee shop yet, and she knew that soon she wouldn't have time for a phone call. She wanted to see if it was important before the rush started.

"Hey, sweetie. I'm not interrupting anything, am I?" her mother asked.

"I'm at work, but I've got a couple of minutes. What's up?"

"I just wanted to know if you've decided who else you're going to invite for Christmas. You only have the one guestroom, and you just know that the motel is going to fill up over the holidays, if it's not already full. If I'm going to have to stay elsewhere, I need to start making plans now. I'm not driving all the way back home after Christmas dinner."

"You don't need to worry. It's just you and Alyssa, and she's leaving in the afternoon to go to her parents'."

"No one else? No special man in your life that you want to spend the holidays with?"

Lorelei rolled her eyes. "You can ask after Hugh directly, you know. And he's going out of town to visit his family on Christmas Eve, but he'll be back before New Year's. I'll see if he wants to come to the party at your place."

"That would be lovely, dear. I'll let you get back to work now. Thanks for calling me back."

She said goodbye to her mother, wondering if the other woman really thought that she would change her mind and kick her out of the guestroom at the last minute. Well, she supposed she might – but only if her mother had something unkind to say about Latte.

CHAPTER SEVEN

Jenny insisted on staying for a double shift, and Lorelei couldn't find it in her to object. She got the feeling that her employee didn't want to be alone just then, she couldn't in good conscience refuse her the sanctuary of the coffee shop. Besides, it felt nice and rather festive to work with her and Mary. They rarely all worked together. Jenny and Mary were her two most experienced employees, so they usually worked opposite shifts, making sure that everything got done correctly when Lorelei wasn't there. Henry didn't need much supervision, though he did have a tendency to gossip, but Norah was still finishing up her training.

They closed early enough on Sundays that while the

sun had started to dip down toward the horizon, it wasn't yet dark out by closing time. It was a nice change, and the soft, golden glow outside gave Lorelei a boost of energy. The three of them locked the doors, then turned the radio up louder and began cleaning the coffee shop to the tunes of old Christmas songs.

"More holidays need music," Jenny said as she mopped. "Just think about it; we could have Thanksgiving music, Easter music, Fourth of July music… It would be great."

"Now that you said it, it is a bit strange that the only holiday that really has its own music is Christmas. Well, I suppose Halloween has some too. I'm sure some of the other winter holidays do as well, but Christmas is the only one I've ever celebrated.," Mary said. She was counting out the register while Lorelei cleaned the windows. The cold outside made the window cleaning solution leave streaks on the glass no matter what she did.

"A bit off topic, but maybe we should do a Christmas in July week this year," Lorelei said. "We can bring out the decorations, play some Christmas music, offer some festive coffee, and just generally boost people's spirits. It might be fun."

"I'd love that," Jenny said. "You should get Norah involved too; she loves decorating. She would probably have some good ideas."

"She mentioned how much she likes decorating after we decorated the coffee shop this year," Lorelei said. "I felt bad for doing it without her; if I'd known how much she enjoyed it, I would have waited for a day she was working too."

She reached the edge of the window and stepped back, frowning at it. The smudges from various fingers and Latte's nose were gone, but there were still streaks if she looked closely enough. She would just have to deal with it for now; the window cleaning solution just didn't want to dry quickly enough when the glass was so cold.

She bent down and picked Latte's bed up off the floor, placing it back in its normal spot on the windowsill, then looked around for her cat. She usually put Latte in her cat carrier when they started cleaning, but they hadn't bothered today; none of them were in a huge hurry, and they were just having fun with it .

PATTI BENNING

And it wasn't just the humans having fun. She smiled when she saw Latte chasing the mop that Jenny was holding. Jenny was giggling, halfheartedly trying to keep the cat away.

"I'm going to start cleaning the coffee machines," she said. "If you get tired of Christmas music, feel free to change the channel. And feel free to leave whenever you want to head home, Jenny. You've already stayed much longer than you needed to. I appreciate it, but I don't want you to feel bad about being late any longer. You've more than made up for it."

"All right, if you're sure. I'll probably get ready to go pretty soon. I do still have to grab some stuff from my apartment before heading to the motel tonight. I'll finish mopping first, though."

Lorelei nodded, then walked over to grab Latte. The cat squirmed in her arms, but Lorelei held her firm. "Let Jenny finish mopping in peace, then you can run around like a little whirlwind again. She'll never get out of here if you don't leave her alone for at least a few minutes."

She headed toward the closet where she kept Latte's carrier while she was at work and opened the door

CLAWS OF MURDER

with one hand. While she was distracted, Latte squirmed out of her grip and ran back over to Jenny, who waved Lorelei off.

"It's fine, she's not too hard to work around. I think she knows I've been upset and is trying to cheer me up; she usually isn't this playful."

"If you're sure. If it gets annoying, let me know. I don't mind putting her in her carrier while we finish cleaning. I'm sure we would all like to get home eventually, and it's hard to do that when she won't let you finish mopping."

Cleaning out the coffee machines wasn't her favorite task at the coffee shop, but there was no avoiding it. She went back and forth, first cleaning the espresso machines, then the large self-serve machines. Once everything was spotless, she checked the task off of her to do list, then tossed all of the used rags and hand towels from the day into the laundry bag, which she closed and put by the door for her to take with her when she left. She would have to run the washer tonight and put the clean rags in the dryer in the morning before coming in.

She heard the bell by the front door jingle and

wondered if Jenny was leaving. She hoped she had somewhere safe and comfortable to go that night. *I should double check,* she thought. *If she doesn't have somewhere safe to stay, she can stay with me. The guestroom's already tidy since Mom is coming over for Christmas, and I wouldn't mind having her stay for the next couple of days until she gets things figured out.*

She moved from the kitchen into the main area and saw Jenny fighting with Latte at the front door. The cat kept trying to dart out, and Jenny kept pushing her back and gently but firmly. Mary was watching, looking amused.

"She's just determined to follow me," Jenny growled. She tried to block Latte with one of her legs as she inched through the door, but the cat pushed her head past and tried to squeeze her shoulder by. Jenny glanced up then, spotting Lorelei.

"She really wants to get outside for some reason."

Lorelei nodded once, hoping that her face didn't betray her emotions. She had a good feeling she knew why Latte wanted to get out so badly. Last time the cat had acted this way she ignored it, and someone had died.

"You can let her out," Lorelei said. "Don't worry, I've got a GPS tracker on her collar. I don't think she'll go far, but if she does, I'll be able to find her."

"Are you sure?" Jenny asked.

"I'm sure. She won't give up until she gets outside. I'll just have to track her down before going home, but that's all right."

"All right," her employee said doubtfully. She stepped back, letting Latte dart out the door. Lorelei watched, expecting the cat to run one way or the other down the street, but instead Latte stopped right outside the door and sat down, staring expectantly up at Jenny.

"I guess you're right, she really didn't go far," Jenny said. She gave Lorelei and Mary a quick smile. "All right, I'll leave now and shut the door, sorry for letting all the cold air in. Thanks for being so supportive today, both of you. I'll see you soon."

She let the door shut and Lorelei watched through the glass as Jenny pulled her hat down further and zipped her coat up higher before putting her hands in her pockets and starting to walk down the sidewalk. Latte followed her, and Lorelei felt as if the world was spinning. Jenny. Latte was following Jenny.

It wasn't until the pair of them vanished past the windows that Lorelei jumped into action. She hurried into the back to grab her coat and her purse, then ran toward the front door while still zipping her coat up.

"What are you doing?" Mary asked.

"I've got to go. Sorry, I can't explain. Can you just make sure to lock up? The only thing left to do is to turn off all the lights."

"I can lock up, but –"

Lorelei didn't hear the rest of her sentence, because she let the front door close behind her and stepped out into the cold. It wasn't snowing, but there was enough wind to pick up snow from the drifts. Tiny shards of ice pelted her in the face as she leaned into the wind, following Jenny and Latte. Jenny didn't seem to be aware that the cat was following her. She had her shoulders hunched and her head down as she walked into the blowing snow. Latte trotted a few feet directly behind her, her ears laid back flat and her fur twitching occasionally at the touch of the snow.

Lorelei quickened her pace, not sure what she should do. Should she call out? Should she make up some excuse and bring Jenny back inside? That might work if Jenny was about to walk into an accident, but if someone was lying in wait for her, all it would do would be to put off the inevitable.

Not for the first time, she wished she could talk to her cat. If only Latte could tell her what she saw or what she knew, then Lorelei's job would be so much easier.

She saw the figure before Jenny did. He stepped out between two buildings, in the same spot where Wilson had been attacked the week before, if Lorelei was remembering correctly. At first, she thought that his head was strangely misshapen, then she realized he was wearing a rubber horse mask, likely left over from Halloween. He had a knife in his hand; large enough that she could see it even from this distance.

Jenny looked up when she was only a few feet away from him, and Lorelei could see the shock go through her. The younger woman froze, but the horse headed figure didn't; he stepped forward, the knife drawn back menacingly.

It all seemed to happen in slow motion to Lorelei. The

second she saw the figure, she pushed her legs into a run, but even though she wasn't far behind Jenny, it seemed like miles. It could only have been a second or two since the figure stepped out from between the buildings, but it felt like an eternity. Any second now, he would lurch forward with that knife and the snow beneath Jenny's feet would be stained red.

"Hey!" she called out as she raced forward. "Stop!"

The horse headed figure jerked his head up, looking at her. She realized that he hadn't seen her before; all of his attention must have been focused on Jenny. He took half a step back, but then his resolve seemed to firm again because he shifted slightly, gripping the knife more tightly and taking another step towards Jenny.

For a moment, she wondered at his determination to kill Jenny even in front of a witness, but then she realized that she wasn't much of a deterrent. The person in the horse mask had the advantage. His identity was disguised, and he was the only one with a weapon against the two of them, one of whom seemed to have had her feet glued to the ground in terror.

But then a car turned at the intersection, coming

toward them. The figure in the horse mask turned his head at the sound of tires crunching over the ice and salt, then backed away into the alley. A moment later, he was gone, and she heard the sound of running footsteps fading away.

Latte, who had her spine arched and her tail fluffed out so much that she looked like a raccoon, relaxed. Lorelei took the last few steps forward and scooped up the cat. Jenny spun around, but relaxed when she saw who it was.

"Lorelei. Thank goodness. Did you see him? I thought… I thought I was going to die."

CHAPTER EIGHT

"And they haven't found him yet?" Alyssa asked.

Lorelei shook her head. "We went back to the coffee shop and called the police, but the person in the mask was long gone. With how windy it was, there weren't even any footprints for them to follow."

"That's so terrifying," her friend said, her eyes wide. "Poor Jenny. How is she doing?"

"She was shaken up, but I think she'll be all right. She's coming in today – she asked if she could pick up an extra shift this afternoon so she doesn't have to be alone all day. I think she's spending time with a friend this morning, but they won't be able to be with her all day."

PATTI BENNING

"I don't blame her for wanting some company right now. I wouldn't want to be alone either, if some crazy person wearing a horse mask was coming after me."

"It has to be about what happened to Wilson, doesn't it?" Lorelei asked, lowering her voice. The coffee shop was empty, but Henry was in the back and she didn't know how much of what happened Jenny wanted to share with the others.

"It's the only thing that really makes sense," her friend agreed. "Unless Jenny has a whole secret life that we don't know about. The person who attacked Wilson must be certain that she recognized him – or her. We still don't even know what gender the person is, do we? You said they were wearing a mask and were bundled up in winter clothes."

"That's true. They were tall according to Jenny so I just assumed they were a man, but I guess it could have been a tall woman as well."

"It must be someone Jenny knows," Alyssa mused. "That must be why the killer thought she recognized them. If it was a complete stranger, they probably wouldn't be that worried about it."

"That doesn't exactly help us much," Lorelei said.

"It's a small town and Jenny works at the most popular coffee shop in it. She knows just about everyone. Plus, she went to high school here, she played sports here, she's lived here her entire life. There must be hundreds of people who she knows well enough to recognize on sight."

"Well, have you asked her? I know she said she didn't get a good look at the person who attacked Wilson, but does she have any gut feelings about them? Something that wouldn't be admissible to the police as evidence, but that she noticed subconsciously, like the way they moved or the way their body was shaped?"

"I haven't exactly interrogated her about what happened," Lorelei said. "It was very traumatizing for her, and I don't want to push her to talk about it if she doesn't want to."

"Well, something's got to happen or else the person is just going to keep coming after her. Oh, I know, maybe we could hire a private investigator like in the movies."

"Sure, but you're paying," Lorelei said. "From what I know, they are very pricey." She spotted someone walking toward the door and nudged her friend, who

PATTI BENNING

was perched on the counter by the register. Alyssa slid off and onto her feet, taking her coffee with her.

"Oh, hey, look who it is," Alyssa said a moment later as Jenny walked through the door. "You're right, it is hard to recognize people with all of their winter clothes on."

"Go sit down somewhere, I don't want her to know that we were just talking about her." Lorelei hissed, trying to shoo her friend away as her employee came closer.

Alyssa just rolled her eyes. "She's my friend too, you know. We worked together. Granted, only for a week or two, but still, we've kept in touch. I have every right to ask her how she's doing. She's not going to shatter like a dropped mug."

Jenny pulled off her hat and her gloves as she approached the counter. She looked tired, but was still in one piece, which Lorelei figured was good news. She'd stayed up late, watching Latte in case the cat got another premonition about Jenny being in danger, but Latte had slept through until morning, curled up happily as a clam on her pillow

"Hey, Alyssa," Jenny said. "I guess you heard what happened?"

"Yeah," Alyssa said. "How are you doing?"

"I keep jumping out of my skin. It's like when you just finish watching a horror movie and you're hyper-aware of every shadow, but worse, because this time I know it's real. Someone really is out there."

"Are you safe in the motel?" Lorelei asked. "I was worried about you all night."

"I have the room closest to the front office, so I should be pretty safe," Jenny said. "I don't think I'm really safe anywhere, though."

"Hey, I have an idea," Alyssa said before Lorelei could say anything. "Why don't you come stay with me until your apartment gets put back together? I've got an extra room. It's a bit cluttered, but the sheets are clean and the bed is comfortable enough. I live in a second-story apartment, so at least you wouldn't have to worry about someone coming in through a window. Plus, my landlord has cameras on the front entrance, so if something does happen, at least the police will have some evidence."

"I don't want to inconvenience anyone," Jenny said. "Or put anyone in danger. That's one of the reasons I'm staying at the motel instead of asking a friend if I can stay with them. It wouldn't be fair to put someone in that position."

"Well, I'm the one asking you. I know all the risks, and I still want you to come stay with me. It would be fun, and I'm sure we'd both feel a lot safer with someone else around. I'm pretty creeped out by all of this too, you know."

"Are you sure?"

"Positive," Alyssa said with a nod.

The first smile Lorelei had seen on Jenny's face since she arrived broke out. "Thanks, Alyssa. I'll grab my stuff from the motel and turn in the key when I'm done here. I'll feel a lot safer staying with you."

"I'm glad. The thought of you staying all by yourself in the motel just gives me the shivers," Alyssa said. "I guess I'd better stop bugging you two now, though. Since you're technically at work, and all."

Lorelei rolled her eyes. "You can stay; it's not like we

have any customers. No one wants to be out in all this wind."

Since they didn't have much to do, and since Jenny hadn't even originally been scheduled for that day, Lorelei was happy to let her and Alyssa commandeer one of the tables and make plans for future specials. Alyssa came up with some outlandish things, and Lorelei was sure she probably wouldn't use most of them, but the list would be a good jumping off point the next time she had to decide on a special.

The wind died down, as it started snowing. Business picked up a little, and within the hour, there was a low hum of conversation in the coffee shop.

Lorelei was in the middle of making an iced mocha – she couldn't help but shoot a glance at the snowy window outside when the woman made that order, but didn't comment; for all she knew the woman just really liked the cold – when a man around Jenny's age came in. He got into line behind the woman Lorelei was currently serving, and it was persistent movement from the table Alyssa was sitting at that caught her attention. Her friend was looking over at her and gesturing with her hands incomprehensibly. Lorelei couldn't make out what her friend was trying to communicate, but Alyssa's gaze was on the man who had just gotten in line.

"There you go, have a nice day," Lorelei said as she handed the mocha to the woman. As soon the woman walked away, Lorelei fixed her gaze on the young man. "Hi, welcome to French Roast. Let me know if you need me to explain anything on the menu."

"I'll try one of those peppermint foam mochas. They sound good," he said.

She took his payment and got started on the mocha. Alyssa was still making strange hand motions, but Lorelei decided to ignore her. Whatever her friend wanted to communicate, she would just have to find a better way to do it.

"Here you go. I hope you enjoy it."

"It looks wonderful, I'm sure I will," he said. He took it, then hesitated, looking around to see if anyone else had gotten in line behind him.

"Is it true that Wilson Belgrove was murdered not far from here?" he asked.

Lorelei's eyebrows rose. "I'd rather not spread gossip. Where did you hear that?"

"He used to be my roommate. One of our mutual friends told me. I was just wondering – it still seems so unreal. Someone mentioned the coffee shop, but I'm not sure exactly what happened."

"You would have to go down the street a bit, but there's nothing there to gawp at."

"I'm not going to sightsee," he said. "I just wanted to, I don't know… Tell him sorry, I guess."

"For what?" she asked, but he was already turning and walking away.

She frowned. At least she knew what Alyssa was trying to communicate now. That man was her across the hall neighbor, the one who'd had such a bad experience with Wilson as his roommate.

CHAPTER NINE

The evening wore on, and Alyssa ended up staying to help out after Henry left, more just to hang out than because they actually needed the extra hands. She'd worked for the coffee shop for a couple of weeks after it first opened, but was an absolute disaster in the kitchen. Still, she knew how to do most of the basic tasks and could help out with cleaning as well as any of them. Lorelei knew that Alyssa already was on Christmas vacation at her job, and she had the suspicion that her friend was bored. Alyssa was the sort of person who always liked having something to do, and didn't handle down time well.

The snowfall kept increasing in intensity as the evening wore on, and the wind picked up again. As

PATTI BENNING

the visibility dropped, so did the number of customers who came in, and it wasn't long before the coffee shop was as quiet as the grave. The occasional customer they did get simply ran inside, braced against the cold, and got something hot before leaving again, in a hurry to get home before the roads got worse.

She was busy giving Alyssa a quiz from a magazine when the bell above the door jingled and she looked up to see Hugh coming in. He pulled his coat off as he came up to the register, nodding at Alyssa, who waved back at him. Jenny was in the kitchen, putting some of the dishes away.

"I hope neither of you are planning on going out tonight. It's terrible out there. I left from the office in the city hours ago, and I'm just getting back now. The highways are completely blocked."

"I was wondering what was going on, usually you are in a lot earlier," Lorelei said. "What can I get you? The peppermint foam mocha again?"

"Definitely, that will hit the spot," he said.

"So, what do you think about everything that is going on?" Alyssa asked as Lorelei got started on the drink.

"You mean about that man being killed?" Hugh asked. "I think it's horrible, and I hope it doesn't have anything to do with the break-in at Jenny's. I'd hate to think that she's in danger."

"You must not have heard," Alyssa said. "Someone attacked Jenny yesterday evening. She just barely got away with her life – Lorelei just happened to chase Latte outside right before it happened and she saw the whole thing. Jenny probably only survived because Lorelei was there; she distracted the attacker long enough to make him pause until a vehicle came down the road and fled. And get this, he was wearing a creepy mask, like something out of a horror movie."

"No, I didn't hear about that," Hugh said. Lorelei heard something slightly off in his tone and looked up to see him gazing at her with a crease between his eyebrows.

"Yeah, it's all thanks to Latte that Jenny is still here, really," Alyssa continued on obliviously. "It's crazy how tiny coincidences like that can change everything, isn't it? If Latte hadn't slipped out the door just then, Lorelei wouldn't have been there to distract the person in the mask, and Jenny might have gotten hurt, or worse."

"Yeah, what a coincidence," Hugh mumbled.

Lorelei finished the coffee and practically shoved it into his hands. "Here you go. It's hot, so drink it carefully. Do you want to sit and chat? It's been pretty slow, I'm even thinking of closing early. I probably will if weather gets worse."

"No, I – I should go," he said. He started walking away, barely seeming to see her.

"Hey, you're forgetting something," Alyssa called. He turned, saw the coat he had left on the counter, and hurried back to get it. He didn't pause to say anything, just turned and, a moment later, went out the door.

"That was odd," Alyssa said, staring after him. "Was it something I said?"

"No, it's not your fault. I think it's about an argument we had a few days ago," Lorelei said, watching him go with concern. Was he upset that she had been involved in another life or death situation? She told him that she would tell him the truth eventually, wasn't that good enough?

"Well?"

She turned her head to look at her friend. "What?"

"Aren't you going to go after him?"

"I'm in the middle of a workday, Alyssa."

"You just said you were thinking of closing early, and no one's here. Plus, Jenny and I can handle it if you're gone for a while. Go."

"Fine, fine," Lorelei said. She hurried into the back to grab her coat and her purse, and went outside after Hugh. Given the weather and the fact that he'd said he had just returned from the city, she figured he'd driven which meant that he would be parked around back, since the road parking had been overcome by snowdrifts. She hurried down the sidewalk and turned the corner. Sure enough, she saw his vehicle pulling out of the lot. She waved, and he pulled over as close to the curb as he could get, stopping and rolling down the passenger window.

"What is it?" he asked.

"Can we talk?"

He nodded, and she heard the sound of the door unlocking. She got in, and waited as he did a quick U-turn and parked back in the parking lot, rolling the window up and leaving the engine running with the heat on.

"You seemed upset when you left," she said.

"I'm just trying to think things through," he said. "I know you said you would tell me eventually. That should have been good enough for me, but I can't stop wondering. I can't just turn my brain off. And I noticed that every time something happens, Latte seems to be involved. The only explanations I can come up with sound crazy. It makes me feel like I'm losing my mind."

"What… what explanations have you come up with?" she asked, her heart pounding. Had he figured it out?

He sighed. "Look, I don't know what I believe, I'm just trying to put impossible pieces together. Don't laugh, okay, but can you talk to her? Is she secretly some sort of super intelligent cat? A government experiment, maybe?"

"No," she said. "Well, she is pretty smart for cat, but she can't talk, and I don't think she's a government experiment."

"But she is involved in some way?"

She nodded, then leaned her head back against the seat and closed her eyes. It made no sense not to tell him. He deserved the truth, and if she didn't tell him now, he would just keep trying to figure it out.

"She can sense death," she said, her heart pounding dully in her throat. She couldn't believe she was doing this. "She always knows when someone is about to die. And I know how it sounds, probably completely insane, but I'm not the only one who has noticed it. She lived at the local nursing home with my grandmother before she came to live with me, and the staff there were the ones who told me about it. I didn't even believe it myself until this summer, which is when all of this started. She can sense when someone is in fatal danger, and when she does, she goes after them, following them around until whatever happens, happens. That's why I got her the GPS collar; with the app on my phone, I can track her down when she goes outside and I can help protect people from accidents or crimes, like what almost happened to Jenny yesterday."

"That sounds crazy," he said, shaking his head. "I believe you, don't get me wrong, but I can see why you didn't tell me earlier. You've really been doing all of that? Saving people's lives?"

She nodded. "How could I not? Once I realized what she could do, using it to help people was the only possible way to move forward. And she seems to like it, too; she's always happy when we save someone, and she gets so upset when someone needs our help."

"Thank you for telling me," he said.

"Are we okay now? Do you have any questions?"

He let out a strange laugh. "I've got hundreds of questions, but right now I think I just need some time to process everything. Like I said, I believe you it's just… I need some time."

"All right," she said. She reached for the door handle. "I'm glad I told you. My mom and the nursing home's director are the only ones who know, other than you."

"I'm glad you told me, too," he said. He gave her a weak smile and she opened the door, stepping out into the cold. She watched as he drove away, feeling simultaneously lighter and more worried. Fewer secrets between them was a good thing, but there was no telling how he would act once he had had time to think about everything. She just hoped that he wouldn't go around telling people. She didn't think anyone would believe him if he did, but what if someone did believe him, it might put Latte in danger.

She began walking back toward the front of the building, her hands in her pockets, and almost didn't see the figure crossing the street at the corner. He slipped on a patch of half frozen slush and she stepped forward to help him. It was only after her hand was already on his arm that she realized who it was.

"Padraic?" she asked.

"Lorelei? I didn't even see you, what are you doing out here?"

"I was just heading back into the coffee shop. You look freezing. You should come in for a cup of coffee."

"That's where I was heading anyway," he said.

She nodded, and they walked together into French Roast. He pulled down his hood and looked around.

"It's slow in here," he said.

"It's the weather," she said. "So, what can I get you?"

"Whatever the special is," he said, his eyes darting around the room. His gaze landed on Alyssa, who was on her phone at one of the tables. Jenny was in the kitchen; Lorelei could hear her humming as she did the dishes.

"It's the same as it was last week. Peppermint Foam Mocha."

"That's good," he said.

She nodded and started making it. He seemed uncomfortable. One of his hands kept drifting to his pocket, and his eyes never stopped shifting around the room. When she finished the drink, she handed it over to him with a warm smile.

"There you go. It's on the house tonight." He looked like he could use it. "I hope things are looking up for you."

"I'm getting by," he said. He wrapped both his hands around the coffee cup. "Thanks."

"If you still haven't found anything by the new year, come see me," she said, relenting. He just seemed so pitiful right now. "I might be able to find a way to fit you in part-time."

"Thank you," he said with more feeling, meeting her eyes. "That actually… That means a lot."

"Of course. I know you've had some rough patches with us, but I want to help if I can."

He gave her a small, tense smile, then nodded toward the door. "I'd better get going. It's just going to keep snowing and blowing all night, and if I wait any longer, the drifts will have covered the sidewalks."

She bade him farewell and watched as he left the building, then turned to Alyssa, gesturing her friend over. "I'm going to get started on cleanup. Will you write up a sign to stick on the door letting people know we closed early due to the weather? There's no sense in staying open during this, and I'd rather everyone gets home safely."

"Sure thing. That will give Jenny and me more time to get her stuff from the motel, too. This will be fun, like a sleepover. Hopefully we don't lose power; if it doesn't go out, we can stay up late watching movies. I think I've got popcorn somewhere in one of the cupboards. It will be a nice, nonthreatening evening."

Lorelei smiled. "I'm glad she's staying with you. Being alone right now wouldn't be good for her."

CHAPTER TEN

It usually only took Lorelei about five minutes to drive home from French Roast, but it took nearly double that that evening. She took to the streets carefully, unable to see more than a few feet ahead of her. She tried turning her brights on, but they just made the snowstorm even more impossible to see through. When she finally pulled into her driveway, it was a relief. She couldn't even see the *For Sale* sign in the next-door neighbor's lawn when she stepped out of her vehicle, let alone Marigold's house. Everything felt strange, like she and Latte were the only beings left in the world.

She took the cat carrier up to her front door and

PATTI BENNING

quickly let them inside. Latte was once again flecked with snow, which she shook off as soon as Lorelei opened the carrier door.

"There you go, you can dry off while I plug my phone in and make sure all the curtains are closed to keep the heat in. Alyssa had a good point; we might lose power tonight, and it's going to be cold if we do."

Worst case scenario, she and Latte could always drive around in the car and let the heater warm them up, but that would be a miserable way to spend the night. If the power went out, she would have to bunk down in the living room with Latte. The gas fireplace would still work, and with the curtains and the doors to the rooms she wasn't using closed, the living room would stay relatively warm. As long as her phone was fully charged, she might be a bit uncomfortable, but she wouldn't be miserable.

She battened down the house, then returned to the kitchen to feed Latte, who dove into her meal right away. The wind howled around the house, making the roof and walls creak and moan. Lorelei shivered despite the fact that the furnace was still running.

Feeling restless and hungry, she decided to put a sandwich together for dinner. She didn't want to take the risk of being caught halfway through making something in the oven or on the stove if the power went out, and it turned out to be a good choice. No sooner had she put the mayonnaise on her sandwich than the kitchen lights flickered, then after a pause, went black.

Lorelei could have sworn that the temperature dropped immediately, as soon as the furnace went off. She picked up her plate and her sandwich and walked over to the kitchen sink, where she looked out the window while she ate. With the lights off inside, the snow outside seemed almost to glow with its own light. *There must be a full or mostly full moon up there above the clouds,* she thought. With the only sound that of the wind, and her visibility so limited, it was an eerie experience.

When she was done with her sandwich, she put the plate in the sink and opened the fridge long enough to grab a can of soda, which she brought into the living room. Her phone was only half charged, which wasn't ideal, but she supposed she could go charge it in her car if she needed to. For now, she unplugged it and spent some time scrolling through her social media accounts while sipping her soda. She wasn't really sure what to do with the evening. She was home earlier than she had expected, but with the power out, she couldn't do most of her chores, at least not easily, and it wasn't as though she could watch something on the television. She couldn't even read, not unless she wanted to prop her phone up and use the overly bright glare of its flashlight to see her book by, or squinted at the pages by the light of candles, both of which would probably end with her getting a headache.

When her phone rang, Alyssa's name flashing up on the screen, she felt a spark of relief. If her friend was about to invite her over, she would definitely accept the invitation. She would much rather spend the evening chatting with Jenny and Alyssa than spend the evening alone with her phone.

"Hey," she said, answering the call and pressing the phone to her ear. "Is your power out too?"

"Yes," Alyssa said, her voice low. "But that's not why I'm calling. Remember Benny? Well, he just stopped by to see if I needed any help, and Jenny absolutely freaked out when she saw him. She told me she thinks he's the one who attacked Wilson. She's locked herself in the bathroom, and he's still in the kitchen. I don't know what to do."

"Are you in danger?" Lorelei asked, all of her boredom gone and sudden worry for her friend and her employee making her heart beat faster. "Do you need me to call the police?"

"That's the thing, I don't actually know if she's right. It was just the hat – she said she recognized the hat he was wearing, but it's just a regular blue wool hat, half the town must have one."

"Can you ask him to leave?"

"I don't want to do anything out of the ordinary. If he really is the person who killed Wilson, he's going to know something is going on and we might be in danger," Alyssa said. "I don't know what to do, Lorelei."

"Do you want me to come over? I can make something up – I can get you and Jenny out of there. The two of you can come to my house. I've got the couch and the guestroom, and the gas fireplace is working."

"Would you?" Alyssa asked. "Thank you. I'd appreciate it. Even if he leaves, Jenny isn't going to be comfortable staying here with him right across the hall."

"I'll be there – just give me about ten minutes."

CHAPTER ELEVEN

She decided to leave Latte at home, both because the cat was asleep and because it would be cramped enough with both Alyssa and Jenny in her convertible without the cat carrier taking up half the backseat. She grabbed her purse, shoved her phone inside, put on all of her winter gear, and left the house, locking the door behind her. Somehow, all of that took almost five minutes, and she felt the pressure of passing time. She had, after some hesitation, shut the gas fireplace off before leaving, not wanting to risk starting a house fire. She knew the house would cool down quickly, but Latte had a pile of blankets to burrow into, she was planning on being back soon. The cat, with her built-in fur coat, could withstand cold a lot better than she would a raging house fire.

It took her longer than she would have liked to get into town. Alyssa's apartment was a couple of blocks away from the coffee shop, and street parking was the closest option, unless she wanted to go down a side street and park behind the building. She got lucky, finding a spot that someone had just vacated so it hadn't yet been snowed in, but the sight of the drifts against the other cars reminded her that she needed to be quick. Her convertible wouldn't do well if she tried to drive it through a mound of snow.

She jogged over to the apartment door and pulled it open. It didn't have a buzzer, but she spotted the *Smile, You're On Camera* sign, and glanced up at the security camera in the corner as she went in.

The apartments were small ones, above the storefronts, and the entrance led to a simple, rickety staircase. With the lights out, the landing above was in darkness. There were two apartments on the top landing, with Alyssa's on the right. Lorelei had been there countless times, but never in a power outage, and the hallway was eerie as she approached the door.

She knocked and affixed a smile to her face. Moments later, the door opened and Alyssa looked out at her, an equally fake smile on her own face.

"Oh, Lorelei," she said too brightly. "What are you doing here?"

"Well, since the power's out, I wondered if you wanted to come over to my house? I've got that gas fireplace, and I can light some candles. We could even pull out an old boardgame. It would be more fun than sitting in here alone with nothing to do."

"Of course, I would love to come over," Alyssa said, sounding like the worst stage actor in the world. She motioned Lorelei into the apartment. "Sorry, Benny. I think we're going to head over to Lorelei's. It will be warmer there."

"Oh, not a problem. I've probably overstayed my welcome anyway," he said, giving her a bright smile. "I'm glad the two of you will be toasty warm."

"Well, I'd better go get Jenny," Alyssa said. "Thanks for thinking to check on me, Benny."

"Anytime." He straightened up from where he was leaning against the counter, and Alyssa hurried down the hall. Lorelei heard her knock on the bathroom door.

PATTI BENNING

"Jenny? Lorelei is here. We're going to go over to her house."

The bathroom door opened, and she heard Jenny and Alyssa talking in low voices. While they conversed, she turned to Benny, who cleared his throat. "You're that coffee shop lady, aren't you?"

"That's right," she said, trying to smile even more widely. "It's nice to see you again."

"You are too. I thought that other girl looked familiar too – she works in the coffee shop as well, doesn't she?"

"You mean Alyssa?" Lorelei asked, being purposefully dense. Her heart was pounding. Was he trying to fish for information about Jenny? "She used to work there, but she hasn't for a while. We've been friends for years, though."

"No, I mean –"

He broke off as a knock sounded on the front door. He and Lorelei exchanged a look. "Alyssa, someone's here," she called out after a moment, when the knock came again. Who would venture out in a storm like this?

"Coming," her friend called back. She appeared a moment later, and hurried to the front door. "It's probably my landlord," she said, reaching for the handle. "She always comes to check –"

She broke off as she pulled the door open and they saw someone wearing a rubber Halloween horse mask standing in the hall.

"Hey, what are you doing here? Who are you?" Benny asked, the first of them to move. He stepped forward, his body language changing from relaxed to confrontational. Lorelei took a half step back, grabbing her friend's wrist and pulling Alyssa along with her. From the looks of it, Jenny had been very wrong about Benny being the killer.

Instead of answering, the person wearing the mask slashed the knife that was gripped in his hand at Benny. Benny jumped back, swearing, and made a grab for the figure's wrist. He was too slow, and on the knife's return, it caught him in the shoulder. Benny stumbled back, giving a wordless shout at the pain as he was driven into the kitchen.

The masked figure turned to her and Alyssa. He

didn't make any immediate moves, but that was when Jenny came down the hallway.

Lorelei heard her footsteps and turned her head reflexively to see the younger woman come into the living room, where she froze. None of them moved for long moments, then Jenny gave a sharp scream and ran back down the hall, slamming the bathroom door. The figure pushed past her and Alyssa, heading after Jenny.

Lorelei moved toward the hall, only to be pushed out of the way again by Benny.

"Hey, where are you going?" Alyssa snapped at him, her voice high with panic.

"I'm going to get my phone to call the police," he said, his hand pressed over the cut on his shoulder. He didn't wait for her to respond, simply shoving his way out of the apartment and going into the one across the hall.

Lorelei and Alyssa exchanged a look, then the two of them hurried toward the bathroom, where the masked figure was pounding on the door. Jenny was keeping up a constant stream of "Go away, go away, go away," on the other side.

"Hey, you!" Alyssa called out. She threw something at him – one of her shoes, Lorelei realized – and it hit him in the head. He turned, staring at them with the mask's blank eyes for a second, then switched the knife to his other hand. The hand that wasn't holding the knife moved toward his coat pocket and hesitated in a gesture that seemed familiar to Lorelei. She remembered that hesitancy, the flutter of the gloved fingers, and she felt her stomach drop.

"Padraic?" she asked. He froze.

"What?" Alyssa asked, straightening up from where she was trying to take off her other shoe to throw at him.

"No," Lorelei said, ignoring her friend and taking a half step back. "You wouldn't –"

But she remembered how Padraic had left shortly before Wilson had, how he would have seen the flash of the man's cash when he paid with a hundred. How desperate he was for a job, to the point where he might do anything to make money. He and Jenny had worked together for a long time. It made sense that he would think that she had recognized him.

He reached up and pulled the rubber mask off, staring

at her with wide eyes. "You weren't supposed to know," he said. "I didn't want to hurt any of you. Please, Ms. French, you have to believe me. Even Jenny, I didn't – I didn't want to hurt her – but then she saw me. What was I supposed to do?"

"Not kill someone," Lorelei said, her fear strangely mixing with disappointment. "You weren't supposed to kill someone. Why did you attack Wilson? Why start all of this? Was whatever cash you found in his wallet really worth it?"

He looked down, shame and embarrassment coloring his face. "I just – I really needed the money."

"I can't believe this," Lorelei said. "I can't believe you. A few nights ago, were you the one stalking me? And what were you planning on doing when you came into the coffee shop earlier today? Were you going to rob us? I worked beside you for months. I gave you so many chances. I didn't think you were the sort of person, Padraic."

"I wouldn't have hurt you," he said. "I was just angry; mad that you wouldn't hire me, mad that you'd fired me in the first place. I saw you walking home and I followed you. I don't even know why. But I wouldn't... I don't think I would have done anything."

"Alyssa," Lorelei said. "Where is your cell phone? We need to call the police."

Her friend jolted beside her and gave a nod, moving toward the kitchen. Padraic broke out of his shock and slid his hand into his pocket, withdrawing a gun. He let the knife fall to the floor as he pointed the firearm at them.

"You're right, I came to the coffee shop today to rob the cash register, but then you offered me a job after the holidays and you were so nice, giving me the free coffee... I changed my mind. I didn't want to hurt any of you, but like I said, I don't have any choice now."

Lorelei froze and hoped that Alyssa did the same behind her. Her friend could be a wildcard, but his finger was on the trigger and one wrong move might make him shoot. Padraic shifted slightly the gun wavering as if he still wasn't sure about harming them, despite his words. They were at a standoff, she realized. He didn't really want to shoot someone that he knew so well, but he couldn't let them go either. He was in too deep – if you had even one witness

PATTI BENNING

walk away, he would be looking at decades of time in prison.

"Padraic —" she started, but then the bathroom door slammed open, catching him in the back. He stumbled forward and the gun slipped from his hands.

Without giving herself time to think, she lashed out, kicking the gun down the hall. He managed to catch himself before going to his knees, and spun around to see Jenny standing in the hall. She must have spotted the knife as soon as she slammed the door open, because she was straightening up, the blade held in one shaking hand. Her face was pale, but her eyes didn't waver as she looked at him.

"I can't believe it was you. I can't believe it. I don't want to believe it. You tried to *kill* me. You broke into my apartment, when just months before, you joined Mary, Norah, and me there to watch the last episode of that show we all like together after work."

"Jenny, I wouldn't have done any of that, but I know that you saw what I did to Wilson. I couldn't take the chance that —"

"I didn't recognize you, you fool," she said, her voice trembling. "I didn't know who you were, I was half a block away and you were wearing a hat and a big coat and you had your hood pulled up. I had no idea it was you."

"I couldn't take the chance." He stepped forward, and she raised the knife, holding it in front of her with both hands.

"Don't," she said. "I don't know what I'll do if you come any closer. I've been so scared this past week – you don't want to test me. There's three of us and only one of you, and I called the police while I was listening to you talk to Lorelei. They will be here soon, so just… don't move." Her hand shook, but she had a steely glint of determination in her eyes. Padraic looked at each of them in turn, then put his hands up.

EPILOGUE

Lorelei's front yard was filled with fluffy white snow. A lot of fluffy white snow.

She leaned on the snow shovel, wiping one of her gloved hands across her sweating forehead as she glared at the driveway. Clearing it was hard work, but Alyssa would be here any minute, and she wanted her friend to be able to park off the road.

"Merry Christmas!"

She looked up at the words and spotted Marigold, who lived two houses down from her, waving at her from her front porch. Lorelei raised a hand and waved back.

PATTI BENNING

"Merry Christmas!" she called back. Marigold's driveway was empty, and she hoped fleetingly that the other woman had plans to see her friends or family later in the day. She didn't particularly like Marigold, but everyone deserved to be with loved ones on Christmas.

She turned back to her work, shoveling the heavy snow off to the sides, and finished just as Alyssa's car came down the street.

Her friend parked beside her mother's vehicle and the two women embraced. Lorelei took the bag of gifts Alyssa had brought with her, and carried them into the house. Alyssa shut the door behind her and paused to pet Latte, who was standing on the counter. Lorelei glared at the cat halfheartedly – she wasn't supposed to be on the counters, but it was Christmas, and she could afford to relax the rules for a day.

"Are you done with the driveway?" her mother called from the living room.

"Yes, Mom," Lorelei called back. "Alyssa's here."

"Well, tell her to hurry up and come sit down. We have to open our gifts before breakfast."

"I swear, whenever Christmas Day rolls around, she turns into an eight-year-old. You know how most parents always say that it's better to give a gift than to receive one? Yeah, she never said that. Getting gifts is her favorite thing in the world." She kept her voice low so her mother couldn't hear her comments to Alyssa.

"I like your mom," Alyssa said with a grin as she stripped her coat and her boots off. "She's never been one to sugarcoat things. Or lie to children for some silly reason. Of course, getting gifts is better – I can't wait to see what you got me."

Lorelei rolled her eyes. "Luckily for you, I'm the sort of person who likes giving gifts, and I can't wait for you to see what I got you either. Come on, let's go put these presents under the tree and you and my mom can start examining your horde. I'll make French toast and bacon for us afterward. I think I've got some potatoes for hashbrowns, too, but I forgot to check before the stores closed yesterday."

"Wait," her friend said, grabbing her wrist as Lorelei started to walk away. "Does she know? About what happened?"

Lorelei nodded. "I told her all about it. I've been trying to be more honest with the people I care about. I don't think she's thrilled that we found ourselves in that situation, but she is proud that we managed to stop him from hurting anyone else. She swears that she always knew Padraic was bad news, but I'm not even sure she ever met him."

"If she really knew he was dangerous without even meeting him, I'd like to know how. None of us knew, and we worked with him for months."

"I just hope Jenny will be okay. It's got to be hard for her – she and Padraic worked together a lot, and even if they weren't close friends, they were acquaintances."

"She'll come around," Alyssa said. "Padraic's lucky that he is going to prison, because he's got a lot of angry people waiting here for him if he ever comes back."

"I don't think he's brave enough to show his face around here again, even if he gets parole in twenty years," Lorelei said, chuckling. "He looked pretty terrified when he realized he was surrounded by three angry women."

"Are you coming, girls?" her mother called out. "Latte and I are waiting. Your cat looks just as excited to open gifts as I am. Poor thing, her owner doesn't even care, does she?"

Lorelei rolled her eyes. "Come on, we'd better join them. When my mom starts teaming up with Latte, you know it's serious. Let's get into the Christmas spirit. We can talk about depressing stuff later; today is a day to celebrate.".

AUTHOR'S NOTE

I'd love to hear your thoughts on my books, the story-lines, and anything else that you'd like to comment on —reader feedback is very important to me. My contact information, along with some other helpful links, is listed on the next page. If you'd like to be on my list of "folks to contact" with updates, release and sales notifications, etc.... just shoot me an email and let me know. Thanks for reading!

Also...

... if you're looking for more great reads, Summer Prescott Books publishes several popular series by outstanding Cozy Mystery authors.

CONTACT SUMMER PRESCOTT BOOKS PUBLISHING

Twitter: @summerprescott1

Bookbub: https://www.bookbub.com/authors/summer-prescott

Blog and Book Catalog: http://summerprescottbooks.com

Email: summer.prescott.cozies@gmail.com

YouTube: https://www.youtube.com/channel/UCngKNUkDdWuQ5k7-Vkfrp6A

And…be sure to check out the Summer Prescott Cozy Mysteries fan page and Summer Prescott Books Publishing Page on Facebook – let's be friends!

CONTACT SUMMER PRESCOTT BOOKS PUBLISHING

To download a free book, and sign up for our fun and exciting newsletter, which will give you opportunities to win prizes and swag, enter contests, and be the first to know about New Releases, click here: http://summerprescottbooks.com

Made in United States
Orlando, FL
26 July 2023